The Lost Realm

Of Magic

By Krystal A. Erbelding

Illustrations by Brittany Shaw

Published by
Landed Among the
Stars Publishing

10 9 8 7 6 5 4 3 2 1

ISBN-10: 0615817408
ISBN-13: 978-0615817408

Acknowledgments

Special Thanks to my editor Joseph C. Baldwin, and to Brittany Shaw for the beautiful cover art and illustrations.

To Dennis Howie

Thank you for encouraging my

creativity.

Table of contents

Chapter One

I have heard tales of a human who never aged, who wandered in the woods just outside our village. These stories referred to a beautiful, pale woman with long, flowing hair who dressed as if she was from a different time. She is always accompanied by a four-legged, winged animal, but, until recently, I believed these stories to be just that, stories.

Well, it seems I am getting ahead of myself. My name is Philomena, but I go by Mena. My father really wanted a boy so he could be named Philip Toivo the seventh. Luckily, my mother started calling me Mena instead of Phil. I live on the outskirts of Selpan with my family. Our house is on top of a hill surrounded by the woods. A little ways down the road lives an older couple that has always loved telling me the stories of the woman in the woods, along with other tales.

So, the other day I was walking home from the neighbor's house when it began to rain. It was not raining that bad at the time, but I knew I should get home before the weather got worse. Instead of walking down the paved road a ways, I decided to cut through the woods and go up the hill to save time.

Halfway through the woods it began to pour.

4

There was no way I would be able to make it up the hill. I could not see through the rain, and the mud under my feet made me slide down the hill. After struggling in the mud for a few moments, I came across a very large moss-covered tree that had a big opening in it. I figured it had been an animal's home over the winter. I ducked inside

to wait for the rain to die
down.

I moved towards the
back of the tree, and then
I slipped and rolled down a
hill. The next thing I knew
I was sitting on a patch of
dry green grass, and the
sun was shining. I picked
myself up and brushed the
dirt and mud off my
clothes. At first, I
thought I had fallen asleep
and was only dreaming.

However, I turned around and saw the same tree that I had gone into up a small hill. Then I pinched myself to see if I was dreaming. It actually hurt, meaning that I most likely was not dreaming.

Chapter Two

Since it was dry, I decided to walk around instead of going back to the tree. I knew I was not in the same woods. The hill did not go up as high, and there was no road in the distance, only a dirt path. I probably should have been freaked out, but I felt safe with the warmth of the sun on my face. I squeezed my hair to wring out the water as I headed down the hill. I came upon a clearing, where a moss-covered stone house sat. The door was just a large animal skin that hung from the frame.

I could not tell if anyone was home, and I was unsure where to knock on a soft door. As I got closer, I called out, "Hello. Is anybody home?" I moved even closer and peeked in the window, and I noticed that the house appeared to be a lot larger inside than it was outside. A red velvet carpet continued down a long hallway. The hallway was lined with lit candles as far as I could see. I figured I would go in and see if I could find anyone.

Brushing the animal skin to the side, I walked through the doorway and into the room. The only things in the room were two small dust-covered wooden chairs on either side of the entrance to the hallway. As I approached the hallway, I noticed that it was not a hallway at all but a very large painting mounted on the wall. However, when I took a closer look, I noticed the flames on the candles were moving. I reached forward to touch the painting, but my hand became part of the painting. Even though I could move my fingers in the painting, it still looked as if it was a part of the painting. I pulled my hand back to make sure I would be able to get out.

Then I stepped through the frame and into the painting.

I began to follow the long hallway. I turned around a few times until I had gone far enough so that I could no longer see the room I just came from. Then I continued walking until I reached another painting at the end of the hall. The painting was of a room similar to the one I had just come from. I reached forward to see if I could get out through this painting, and my hand looked normal again so I continued to step through. I assumed I had just ended up back in the same place since the chairs were identical to the ones I had seen. Once in the room I continued out the doorway.

Chapter Three

When I got outside, I realized I had been in a different building. The first thing I saw when I walked out the door was a giant gray and white stone castle. It looked like a castle one would find in a fairy tale, with waving banners and tall walls surrounded by a moat. The large wooden drawbridge to the castle was down, so I walked across and came upon two guards. At least I assumed them to be guards. There in front of me stood two enormous snow-white wolves with large feathered wings. I stood in awe, staring up at the two creatures that loomed over me.

I could not decide whether I wanted to run for my life or reach out to pet one. Then I heard a voice greet me, "Welcome, stranger." I looked around to see who was speaking to me until I realized the voice had come from the creature on my right. My eyes grew wider and my jaw dropped as I stared at the creature until the other one spoke, "Maybe she cannot speak."

I stammered a little as I tried to get the words out. "No, no, I mean yes, I can speak. I'm sorry. I'm just not used to animals speaking. I don't mean to stare, but I have never seen an animal like you before." They chuckled for a moment, and then the one on the right spoke again, "It's all right, you seem strange to us in those clothes."

Both of them bowed, then the one on the left spoke, "Welcome to Aerwon. We are wovels, guardians of the Western Gates. If you follow the path ahead you will reach the town." I thanked them both and headed on my way.

Once I passed the wovels, I pinched myself again just to check that I was awake. As I winced a little from the pain in my arm, I came upon an open area filled with townspeople. They were bustling about, going in and out of buildings. At this point, I realized I truly was not dreaming. I had somehow found myself in a hidden world. Some things were similar to what I knew to be normal, but others were very different. The residents of the town were unlike what one would expect to find. Much like the castle, many of them looked like the people or creatures found in fairy tales. One thing I did notice is that they seemed peaceful.

Chapter Four

I stood and watched the people in awe as they went about their day. As I watched all these different species living in peace, I noticed a person who looked human. She was a little over five feet tall with long, wavy jet-black hair and a pale complexion. She wore an elegant, ankle-length dark-green dress with silver trim around her waist. I decided I should try to find out something about this town aside from its name. I approached the woman, and as she greeted me with a hug, she said, "Welcome, stranger. My name is Anna. If there is anything you need, just ask."

I smiled and said, "It's nice to meet you Anna, my name is Mena. Is this place real? Where am I? How did I get here?"

She laughed and replied, "Yes, this place is real. You are in Aerwon, the main city of the realm of magic. You got here through an opening in the magic barrier."

While she talked, I began to think she was not human after all. When I looked at her feet, they were backwards. "Anna, I don't mean to be rude, but you're not human, are you?"

She smiled at me as she responded, "No, I'm not, I am an abarimon. I am similar to a human but my feet face the opposite direction, and I can run at greater speeds than a human can. Actually, as far as I know, you are the only human in our realm, right now."

"But you know of humans?"

"Yes, there was once a time when we all lived among humans. However, magic started to get weaker as everyone began rejecting it. Also you are not the first human to enter our realm."

"So those wovels I met when I entered the western gate are real?"

"Yes they are. I'm sure you're not used to seeing creatures like them but, don't worry, we are all, for the most part, peaceful."

As Anna continued talking, I began to look around at all the other species. "Chances are any creatures you have heard of in stories are here." I turned and looked at her, "There is a story in my village of a woman who never ages that runs through the woods with a winged beast. Does she live here?" "Yes that is Amara. She gets restless sometimes and wants to see humans to see if they are ready?"

"What do you mean ready?"

"Don't worry about that now, everything will be explained. I must be off but feel free to look around; just stay inside the walls. We don't want anything to happen to you." I began to ask her what she meant when she disappeared.

Chapter Five

I was so mesmerized by the thought of all of this being true that I had not realized that many residents were staring at me. When I glanced in their direction, they began to go about their business. I figured, while I was here, I should at least take a look around and meet as many of the creatures as I could. After a quick glance, I saw some creatures I recognized from stories; there were satyrs, elves, gnomes, centaurs, and a cyclops, along with many others. I think I may have even seen Pegasus. At that point, I glanced up, and, for the first time, noticed dragons and fairies along with other creatures flying about. Fascinated by everything around me, I continued to look around the town. The streets were lined with shops and homes as far as I could see; one in particular, caught my eye: "Human Tales Library." I assumed that meant they know our stories about them.

I began to walk down what appeared to be the main street until I found a wooden sign in the shape of an arrow pointing to a path, which read "To Lake Ichtaca." I followed the path when I came upon a large creature that had a body similar to a horse with the head and neck of a dragon and antlers of a deer; it also had a long flowing yellow mane that looked almost as if it was on fire. It was eating some fruit from the trees along the path. The creature turned its head and smiled at me. "Greetings, stranger; would you like a pear?" he asked.

Still shocked at the fact that animals were talking to me, I paused for a moment then said, "Yes thank you. My name is Mena, what's yours?" I grabbed a pear from the tree as he responded, "My name is Chip. You're human aren't you? Well, I mean, of course, you're human. I'm sorry you are probably confused; I'm a kirin." I smiled at my new fast-talking friend and asked if he could tell me about the realm. He said, "Sure I can. I am going to the lake; do you want to come with me? I can give you a ride if you don't want to walk. It's just up the road a little ways. Do you want to join me?" I agreed to join him on his way to the lake but passed on riding him. I grabbed another pear as we continued on. "Can you tell me how this place came to exist?" I asked.

As we walked, he told me that many years ago, magic was being rejected, and many of the creatures were forced into hiding because people wanted to capture them for one reason or another. Some would do it for sport; others for fame. So, the leaders of all magical creatures gathered together to create a realm where they could all live without fear of being captured. Residents of the realm could go out into the world occasionally, but humans could not get in until there was a chance that the world would be ready for magic once again. He also informed me that I apparently was the one person who would be the test to see if the world was ready.

"Are you telling me that it depends on me if magic reenters the world?" I asked. He stopped, looked at me for a second, and said, "Yep, yep." Then he continued down the path with me just a few steps behind.

Chip

Chapter Six

Once Chip and I reached the lake, I saw something that looked very familiar. I turned to Chip in shock and asked, "This may sound odd, but is that Nessie, the Loch Ness monster?"

"Not quite," he responded, "but she is her kin that is her granddaughter. She had a few children. That's why a lot of the sightings in your world were slightly different."

"I thought that this place was created a long time ago."

"It was but like I said we can travel to your world. Ever wonder why no one ever captured Nessie or got proof of her existence? It's because she never stayed too long."

I sat down on a log near the lake as Chip drank from the lake. I peered out across the water and saw mer-people watching the sun as it began to set. By this time, Chip had rejoined me. I looked up at him from the log and said, "I see dolphins in the water just off shore. I don't understand dolphins; are not mythological beings."

"Sometimes animals come and go as they please, but that's not exactly a dolphin that's an encantado. It looks like a dolphin during the day, and it stays deep in the water; at night they come on land and look like humans with big foreheads. Oh no, no, no, no! We best be off; you shouldn't stay here; it's getting late if they see you. Oh no, no! Climb on! I'll explain on the way. We must go!"

I climbed upon his back and was surprised that his scaled neck was softer than I had thought it would be; I held on tight as he took off. "Encantado's kidnap humans and sometimes make them sick. I don't want you to get sick. We can't have that."

Once we reached the pear trees, I climbed down as Chip urged me to go on ahead in case they noticed me. He would stay, just in case, and keep them back. I turned and ran back to the shops.

Chapter Seven

There was a large clock
in what I assumed was the
town square. The clock
chimed as it was turning
nine o'clock. I had to get
out of there; I had to go

home. I headed back through the west gate and past the wovels. I yelled out to them, "Good-bye friends, I'll see you tomorrow!" as I headed toward the direction of the small stone house. After I got out of sight of the wovels, I slowed down. It was very dark at this point. There were no streetlights, so I was relying only on moon light which was not very bright. All of a sudden, I stopped as I thought about what Anna had said before she vanished. She warned me to stay within the walls. I shrugged it off; she probably did not want me to get lost. I followed the path until something grabbed my shoulders. Suddenly, I was in the air. I began to scream as I was lifted higher and higher into the air. Then a deep raspy voice came from above me saying, "If you do not keep quiet, I am will have to drop you."

After we flew over the forest and away from the small stone building and the town, a line of mountains became visible in the distance. The creature that had hold of me set me down inside a large opening in the middle of a mountain. As soon as the claws were removed from my shoulders, I ran into the cave as far as I could. Since it was dark inside the cave, I could not see anything and ended up slipping on some loose rocks and hitting my head against the wall.

Chapter Eight

When I came to, I was
unsure how long I had been
knocked out. I knew it had
been a little while at
least because there was a
small fire about four feet

away from me. I got up from the ground and walked closer to the fire to warm up. My head was throbbing from hitting the wall. I reached up to feel where my head had hit the wall and found a bandage on my forehead.

I looked around the cave to see if I could see the creature that had kidnapped me, and, in the distance, near the mouth of the cave, sat a large, furry brown winged creature and what looked to be a short muscular woman. I could not see their faces from where I was sitting but could overhear them talking about me. The large winged one said, "We need to destroy the building, so she can't get out of here."

"But if we do that you know anyone outside of town will be blamed," she said.

"We need to make it look like it was done from the other side so it looks like she did it to protect the world from the monsters that live here."

"However there are other ways out of the realm; someone could go and see if she..." right then the fire crackled and both of them turned to look. The winged creature did not have a neck. His head made me think of an owl, and his arms were wings. He had large, shiny red eyes; his nose and mouth were hidden beneath the fur on his face. The woman had red hair back in a thick braid; she looked like a human woman, just with rougher features. Next to her was an open bag with bandages and food. She looked at me and asked, "Are you hungry?" Figuring she would not bandage me up just to poison me, I nodded my head yes. She stood up, grabbed the bag, and walked closer to the fire. She sat down, set the bag between us, and motioned for me to go ahead. I peered inside and saw fruits, vegetables, and bread. I grabbed a large roll and began to eat it.

When I looked up at the creature at the mouth of the cave, I caught one last glimpse of him as he turned and flew away. The woman spoke once again "I'm sorry about all this. My name is Valina, I am a dwarf. The man who just left was Trank a mothman. He's not as bad as he seems."

"Why am I here?"

"Not everyone wants the magic world and the human world to mix. Some feel that magic is better on its own and humans would only ruin what we have."

"But what does that have to do with me? I did not ask to come here; I did not know what was going on. All I did was crawl into a tree to avoid getting soaked from the storm. I was trying to go home because I'm sure my family is worried about me by now."

She reached over and placed her hand on my shoulder "You are a kind-hearted person who doesn't judge people by how they look and are very open minded. It's been foretold that someone with these qualities will come into the realm and show how much humans have changed and that there is a chance that we could live in peace with one another."

I leaned against the wall, "What's going to happen to me now that Trank or whatever you called him has brought me here?"

"He is going to destroy the way you got here. I'm not sure what's going to happen to you, but I have been assured you will not be harmed."

I reached up to my head as I said, "Too late, but thanks for the bandage."

Chapter Nine

I felt the sun shining
on my face as I awoke. I
opened my eyes and then sat
up quickly. I was still in
the cave. It was not a
dream. I looked around to

see if Valina or Trank were anywhere to be seen. No one was at the mouth of the cave. The fire was no longer burning; it had been put out. Next to me was a large cup of water and a plate full of sliced fruit and a roll. I had not had anything to drink since I got here, so I gulped the water down before eating the food. I peered out the cave and stepped back

quickly when I realized
just how high up I was.
When looking out I saw a
large forest that stretched
for miles and a few bodies
of water here and there.
The longer I stared out,
the more I thought about
all that had happened and
about the creatures I had
encountered. Suddenly, I
got an idea. From what I
could remember from
stories, dwarfs live in

caves. Maybe there is another way out of here.

I got back up and headed to the back of the cave, making sure not to fall on the loose rocks. I kept to the right side of the cave looking for an opening of some sort. I kept going back further and further, keeping one hand on the wall next to me and another out front to prevent me from walking into a wall. Soon I felt that there was a gap on the right-hand side. The opening was wide but not too tall. I crouched down to go down the tunnel. As I followed it, I came upon a staircase. I carefully walked down the stairs and came upon a large room with two large lit torches on the wall, along with five small torches that were not lit. Luckily, this room was tall enough for me to stand up straight. I took one of the small torches and lit it from one of the larger ones. I then looked around to find another tunnel. There were two openings, one next to the opening I had just come out of, and another on the other end of this room. I checked the one on the opposite end of the room since it was closer to me at the time, but that staircase led upwards. I proceeded to the other opening and found that it led down. Wanting to get out of there, I followed the staircase down.

The stairs continued down in a back and forth pattern with landings about every fifteen steps. After going down about twenty flights, I reached an even larger room. This room had

many torches on each wall
and three long stone tables
with benches on either
side. There was a large
door in the center of the
wall opposite me. Looking
around quickly to see if
anyone was around but not
seeing anyone, I ran to the
door. In order to attempt
to open the door, I had to
drop the torch I was
carrying. I grasped the
large handle and tried to

pull the door open, when I heard footsteps. I turned to hide under a table, but it was too late. I had been spotted.

Chapter Ten

Standing before me were two dwarfs, a male and a female. They looked like Valina but were shorter and less muscular. The male spoke "Don't be afraid my name is Athic, and this is my sister Morgunn. We are here to help; come this way."

They started to walk to a wall that had no door. The girl pushed on a rock that caused a door to open in front of them. "Quickly before you are seen." She said. I picked up my torch and followed them into the doorway. Once we all passed through the door, it closed behind us. We walked along the hallway until we came to another room, that was much smaller than the one we had left. I stopped in the doorway to the room.

"Could you please tell me what is going on?" I asked.

"We're sorry, but we didn't want you to get caught. You met our mother last night," he said. "She was helping those who wanted to keep people out of our world."

The girl stepped forward as she spoke, "But she found out that they planned on killing you, and she never agreed to that. There is a way out of the mountain, but, once you get out of here, there is no turning back. Our mother is going to help you get to the city. Wait here, and she will be here as soon as she can."

I thanked them as they each gave me a hug, then left through the same hallway. There was a holder on the wall in the room for a torch, so I placed the one I had been carrying and waited for Valina to come.

Chapter Eleven

It felt as if hours had passed as I sat and waited for her to come. Then, there was a shuffling noise in the hall. I stood up and there in the doorway stood

Valina. "Hello human. What is your name, so I may stop calling you that"?

"It's Mena."

"Well Mena lets get you out of here."

"Valina, why are you helping me?"

"I thought they would take you to another opening and send you home. However, the others do not intend to do so; they want to frame you and say you attacked us, then claim they killed you to save us." I put my hand on her shoulder as I thanked her for helping me. "Here" she said as she handed me a brown hooded-cloak. "Put this on; it will at least hide you from a distance." I put it on and followed her as she led me out another small passageway.

We continued down the hall and came upon a stone

door. She opened the door and motioned for me to go out. I exited the door, and she followed behind, closing the door. "We are many miles from the city. I recommend we get you there as fast as we can. I will go with you as far as I can."

"Won't the mothman notice I'm gone?"

"Not until nightfall; he sleeps during the day,

so we must get as far as we can before that happens."

We headed to a path that led straight into the woods. As we walked in, I noticed it did not look like the woods I was used to at home. Some trees looked lit up as if they were apartments for small creatures.

"Does anyone live in these trees?" I asked as

our paced slowed from a run to a walk.

"Yes, pixies, fairies, nymphs, gnomes, tree elves, mahomanays, mangmangkits, and many more, but those are just the ones that live in the trees themselves. There are many more species that live in the forest. Just a few are unicorns, chimeras, werewolves, and werecats." Trying to picture all the species she named, I became nervous; maybe one of these creatures she named would try to kill me.

As we continued walking something started flying around my head. I was about to shoo away whatever it was until it said, "So you're the human that everyone is talking about. You're a kid."

"I am not a kid. I'm thirteen; why don't you

hold still long enough so I can see you?"

Just then, a fairy appeared hovering right in front of me. He was about seven inches tall with sparkling blue and green wings.

"Mena this is Reedstaff. He knows these woods better than anyone I know," said Valina

"You can call me Reed," he said as he stretched his

arm out for a handshake. Smiling, I shook his hand with my index finger.

"It's nice to meet you, Reed."

The three of us continued on until the path suddenly stopped. Reed started to fly to the left, stopped, and turned around, "We have a choice; we can go around the lake or the swamp; your choice."

"Let's head to the lake; that way by the time it is dark we can make camp near drinkable water," Valina responded.

There was no clear path, so we moved slower as we moved through the trees, over the roots, and ducking branches. Reed kept flying ahead and coming back after he found the best route around some of the trees. He had no problem going straight through since he was small and could fly. However, he had to take into account for our height differences.

While walking I asked, "Valina, you mentioned species that live here in the forest. I have heard of many of them before, but there were a few I have never heard of. Can you describe mahomanays and mangmangkits to me, please?"

"Mahomanays are fair-skinned, human-like creatures. They are the guardians of all animals. Mangmangkits live in trees. They guard the trees here. No one may cut them down without their permission. They look like the mahomanays, except their skin looks like tree bark."

Just then, we came upon a clearing with a small lake. "Let's make camp just inside the tree line, so we can keep you out of sight," said Reed.

"Reed, can you show me where there is food, so we can eat?" asked Valina.

"This way," replied Reed, as he flew away.

Just before Valina left she said, "We will be back

soon. Stay hidden." I nodded as they entered the clearing.

Chapter Twelve

The sky grew darker as I sat and waited for them to return. I curled up against the tree, looking back at the part of the forest from where we had just come. Throughout the forest, it looked as if it was filled with small lights that stopped about twenty feet from the edge of the clearing. Suddenly, I heard a branch snap behind me. I jumped behind a tree and peered out only to see Reed and Valina return with fruits. I thanked them as I was handed what looked like a purple apple. Not having eaten since the morning, I did not question what I was about to eat. I bit into it, and, to my surprise, it tasted like a grape, only with the texture of an apple. "This is delicious. What is it?" I asked as I reached for another.

"It's a grapple," replied Valina.

By now, we were all thirsty, and, because we

had no cup with us, we had to go to the lake directly to get anything to drink.

"Keep your hood over your face just enough so you can see where you're going," Reed said, as we entered the clearing. They motioned for me to get something to drink, and I did. As I was drinking, I heard a voice I had not heard before. It was deep and rough, "Have any of you seen a human wandering about?"

They both responded, "No."

"What about your friend?" he asked as he moved towards me.

Valina was quick to respond. "Sadly, she hasn't seen anything at all. She is an elder elf. She lost her sight a long time ago.

We are helping her to return home."

Just then, I felt a large hand on my shoulder as the voice said, "Sorry my friend." Then I heard him gallop away. I turned just in time to see that it was a very large centaur.

We all moved back into the woods but not before I saw what looked like two shooting stars. "Those stars are beautiful," I said.

"Those are not stars, they are phoenixes," Reed said.

"But they are two different colors, I thought a phoenix looked like fire."

"Some do," he said, "but the blue one is a frost phoenix and the yellow one is a spark phoenix."

"All right, so there are a lot more types than I thought," I said in awe, as I lay down and stared up at the part of the sky I could see through the trees and drifted off to sleep.

Chapter Thirteen

When we woke up in the morning, we all ate some fruit, got a drink of water, and were on our way. We continued along the shoreline enjoying the bright sun upon our faces.

Once we reached the other side of the lake and entered into the forest once again, Valina suddenly stopped. "I must go back," she said, "If I am gone too long my children will be at risk." She handed me a green scaled satchel that she had been wearing over her shoulder. "I wish I could say I will see you again, but, if anyone found out that I have helped you escape, I will be killed. Please, take care of yourself. Reed will continue to lead you out of the forest." I hugged her and thanked her for all that she had done and watched as she headed back from where we came.

"All right Reed, let's get going." I said as I slipped the satchel over my shoulder and wiped the tear from my eye at the parting of a new friend.

Reed continued flying ahead and finding the best route for me to take until he flew out and never came back. I sat on a fallen tree and waited. To kill the time I looked in the satchel that Valina had given me. Inside I found some fruits, rolls, and a note. On the outside it said, "READ WHEN ALONE."

Seeing I was alone, it seemed like a good time to open it up.

Dear Mena,

I am sorry I could only get you part of the way back to the city. However, I feel I must warn you that, if at any time something seems off or something happens to Reed, do not stay put. By now, there is a chance that spies have seen Reed or myself with you. At the bottom of this bag is a compass.

If you must move on your own,

follow the compass south. It will

take you deeper into the woods.

Look for a mahomanay.

Remember they are pale human-

like creatures that live in trees. I

have sent word through a

trusted gnome that you are in

the woods. Also, beware of any

white wisps you run into in the

woods. They are called will o'

wisps; they are completely

neutral but constantly lead

people to get lost in the woods.

Please take care of yourself. I will send word to Aerwon, if I can, that you are still here and in need of help.

Be Safe.

Valina.

I sat there on the tree a little longer as I ate a few pieces of fruit. Then I began to dig into the bag to find the compass. I put the letter back in the bag and started to head south. I thought about being alone in a magical realm where some residents want me dead simply because I am human. By now, my parents are probably worried sick about me.

I continued through the trees trying to move in a straight line as best I could. All the while, I was looking at each tree to see if there was a possibility of a mahomanay living within it. Because of this,

I was moving a lot slower than I wanted to. I came upon a river that I had to cross. I looked around to see if there was a bridge of some sort to get across, but I did not see one right away. I saw a few white wisps in the distance, so, to avoid them, I walked the other way along the river. I followed the river, and, just as it began to rain, I found a small stone bridge that was covered with moss

and vines.

Chapter Fourteen

I got to the middle of
the bridge when all of a
sudden a small green
creature with long pointed
ears popped up in front of
me. I assumed it was a

bridge troll. "Is there a reason you are standing on my home stranger?"

"I am trying to get to the other side of the river."

"Good enough. However, come inside for now so you may stay warm and dry."

I wasn't planning on staying, but the rain was picking up, along with the wind. I followed the troll back down the bridge and to

a door located within the

stone of the bridge.

Once inside I saw what looked to be a normal living room, just a little smaller. There was a lit fireplace, two armchairs with a small coffee table in between them, a love seat across from the two chairs. Atop of the fireplace there were a few picture frames. Each picture was of another troll. "Have a seat," he

111

said as he motioned to the love seat.

"You have a lovely home," I said as I sat down. I kept my hood up, knowing I could claim to be an elf as long as my ears remained hidden.

"Would you like something to eat?"

"I'm fine but thank you," I said as I motioned to my satchel. We sat there in silence waiting for the rain to stop when, suddenly, it sounded like someone was at the door.

He jumped up and pulled the rug to one side. "Quick!" He whispered as he lifted up a hidden door in the floor, "Get in quickly." I couldn't really argue. I went down the stairs into the hidden room as the door shut behind me. I sat and listened as he opened his front door.

"Good day brother," said the troll.

"Good day," the man at the door said. "The rumors are true there is a human somewhere in the woods."

"Does anyone know where the human is or what it looks like?" asked the owner of the home.

"All we know is it is a human female, with dirty blonde hair. She was being held in the mountains until a dwarf helped her escape and met up with a fairy; however, both have been captured and are being held."

"Won't they give any information as to where the human is?"

"No. They won't say a word."

"I will keep an eye out, and, if I see her, I will send word directly to you."

"Good. I must be off to warn the others."

The door opened and closed. Then, there was nothing, silence. A few moments later, the hidden door opened, and the troll popped his head down. "It's safe to come up," he said. I crept up the stairs as he said, "You'll be safe here for a while, but I wouldn't go outside yet, if you do they will capture us both."

"How did you know I was a human?"

"I've been in the human world and have seen what humans look like."

"Thank you for hiding me; do you know where they are keeping my friends."

"No, I'm sorry I don't."

"You're not like the trolls I have heard about in stories."

"Ah, yes the mean old trolls who want to steal from you when you cross their bridge. No. I'm not, but I do know some that are like that. Not all trolls are the same."

The two of us sat there talking for hours about human stories of trolls and troll stories of humans until we noticed it had gotten dark out. "You're welcome to stay here," he said.

"I really should go. I am supposed to find a mahomanay. You don't know where any of them live do you?"

"Actually, I do, and she would help you. Continue south until you come to a clearing with a small pond. Once you get there, go to the other side of the pond, and enter the trees again; her tree should be around there."

"Thank you."

"No, thank you. If you can unite our worlds, I will be very happy. Now a few moments after you leave, I am going to sound the alarm and send them north to try to give you as much time as I can."

I knelt down, hugged, and thanked him for all that he had done. Then I slipped out the door and continued across the small stone bridge.

Chapter Fifteen

The moonlight glistened off the water from the rain that was everywhere which made it a little easier to see. I continued to head south through the trees and into the clearing the troll had told me about. When I reached the pond, I planned to stay long enough to get a drink of water until I saw a large centaur with a family of trolls standing at the edge of the pond. I ducked behind the nearest tree and waited for them to leave. I peeked out from behind the tree to see if they had started to leave, but they were still in the same spot. I began moving around the pond but stayed in the trees. When I was near the end of the clearing, I noticed the centaur and the trolls leave in the direction I had originally been hiding. I quickly moved into the clearing and drank a little from the pond and then continued on.

As I moved further in past the tree line, I

noticed that the trees in this part of the forest were further apart from each other and that the trees themselves were giant red woods. I walked among the trees, and then realized I did not know how to find which tree the mahomanay was living in. I found a large rock and decided to sit for a little bit. For the first time since I had been kidnapped,

I actually sat and thought about what had happened. I had been so worried about staying alive that I had not worried too much about getting home. I know my family will be all right, but they will be worried sick about me. I want to get home. However, I cannot leave my friends that I have made here to be punished for helping me.

As I sat there thinking to myself, something moved in front of me from one side to the other very quickly. I jumped up off the rock when I suddenly felt a hand on my shoulder.

Chapter Sixteen

When I turned around, standing before me was a beautiful pale woman with long flowing red hair, wearing a long white dress with flowing sleeves.

Standing next to her was a small man with rosy cheeks, a gray beard and a tall pointed blue hat.

"Don't worry Mena, my name is Amara. Valina sent my little friend here to let me know you were coming." Just then, the gnome disappeared. "Don't mind Scoot, he is shy around humans." She looked me up and down as she said, "Let's get you out of those clothes and into something a little less human."

I looked at what I had on and realized mythical creatures probably do not wear jeans and a t-shirt. I probably stand out like a sore thumb. Amara led me to a large tree a few feet away. She tugged on a small branch, and a door opened. We walked in, and the door shut itself behind us.

The room was larger on the inside than on the outside. There was a hallway that led into an elegant living room with two large red velvet couches with a glass table in between. Pictures lined the wall of all different kinds of animals. Amara motioned to a room that was off of the living room as she said, "I hope it fits." I walked into the room and saw a canopy bed draped with white sheer curtains. Laid out on the bed was a beautiful sapphire blue dress that looked similar to Amara's except that it had a hood attached to it. I changed into the dress and put my regular clothes and the cloak Valina had given to me in the satchel. When I left the room, Amara looked at me and tilted her head. "One more thing," she said, as she handed me a pair of shoes to match the dress, "Where are you from?" she asked as she poured me a cup of tea.

"I'm from Selpan." I said as I sat down and picked up the cup of tea.

"Oh I know that place well. I love the forest there."

"I've heard stories about you wandering the forest with an animal."

She smiled as she responded, "Yes I am normally accompanied by one of the smaller wovels." She headed to the door as she said, "Well it's about time we get you back to Aerwon, so we can find a way for you to get home."

"I can't go back yet." I said. She turned and stared at me as I continued, "Valina and Reed were captured just for trying to help me. I cannot just leave and forget about them. I want to and have to help them."

"Are you sure? You could be captured again."

I stared into my cup as I said, "Yes. They helped me, now I must help them."

"All right! They are probably not going to be anywhere in the woods. They would be found to easily that way, but I am not sure where they would be. We have to get you out of the woods. Then we can get some help. Are you all right to head out now?"

"Yes," I said as I put the cup down and grabbed my satchel.

Chapter Seventeen

We left her tree and continued south. We did not try to move very fast through the trees because Amara felt that it might make us look suspicious. As

137

we walked, we passed some animals along with other residents of the forest. "If a satyr tries to talk to you just nod and keep walking. Many of them are big flirts," Amara whispered as we walked past a large gathering of satyrs.

I nodded as I pulled my hood further in front of my face. The satyrs just waved as we passed by them. They seemed to be very excited about something. When we were clear of the satyrs I asked, "Amara, what were they so excited about?"

"They heard that a human came into the realm, and they are happy at the prospect of being able to go back into your world." She said as we moved towards the end of the forest.

When we came to the edge of the forest, we began to follow the path heading east that had a sign that read "Aerwon." "I thought we were not going back to the city," I said.

"We're not. We are going to the wovels' den. It's located in a gully up ahead."

We continued on as the sun started to rise reaching the gully just after dawn. Looking down in the gully, I saw many wovels, some white like the ones at the gate, and others were gray, brown, black, red, or mixed. Amara looked back at me as I stood at the top of the gully, "Don't worry; they won't hurt you. They are very kind creatures."

"I am not worried, just in awe of them. They are beautiful creatures."

I started down into the gully when a small wovel, about the size a house cat, ran up to me and followed me down the hill. Once we reached the bottom of the gully, we were surrounded by wovels. Meanwhile the little one was still right at my feet. I bent down and picked him up as he started to lick my face. Amara walked up to one of the larger ones and whispered into her ear. She nodded and then said, "Welcome Mena, my name is Ricarda. We are happy to help. Our friend Mim located where your friends are being held. If you are ready to go, we can head out"

"I'm ready whenever you are."

"All right! Amara, you'll ride with me, Mena you'll ride with Ultan."

As she spoke, a large snow white male walked forward. I put the small wovel down and then got settled on Ultan's back. Meanwhile, Amara was getting herself settled on Ricarda's back. Ultan turned his head and said in a very deep voice, "Hold on." I gripped tightly onto his fur, and then we were off.

We rose high up above the gully and began to fly towards Aerwon. In spite of the distance, the stone walls still looked very large. We flew over the wall, and above the town. When I looked down, I could see the tops of the buildings, stone streets, and even the lake that Chip had shown me. As we continued over the other end of the city, I saw a large lake surrounded by an even larger forest. Running through the forest was a river. We followed the river until it ended. Just below us was a very large waterfall.

"Your friends are being held behind the waterfall in a cave," said Ricarda.

"We can get you to a ledge in the cliff just to the side of the waterfall, but from there you are on your own," added Ultan.

Ultan and Ricarda moved close to the ledge on the cliff, which was only about a foot deep. Amara and I slipped off of our friends' backs and landed on the ledge. They nodded as they flew away. "Stick as close to the wall as you can," advised Amara as she moved closer to the falls. I followed behind her, slowly sliding my way along the side of the cliff. When we reached the edge of the falls, Amara slid her way behind it and into the cave. I moved closer and began to go behind the falls when my foot slipped on the slick rock. I would have fallen except for the fact that Amara grabbed my hand just in time. She pulled me up into the cave, and I sat there staring at

the falls for a moment.
"Thank you," I said as I
began to wring the water
out of my dress and hair.
She smiled and helped me to
my feet.

Chapter Eighteen

The cave was wet from the spray of the falls, which made the ground very slick. We stuck close to the walls until we reached where it was dry. The cave was lit by torches on each side spread out about every four feet. A little ways off I saw a space with no torch. I motioned to Amara, and she nodded, letting me know she saw it too. Once we reached the space, we noticed it was a hallway that wasn't lit. "I'll go this way, if you want to continue going on the main hallway," whispered Amara. I nodded and handed her a torch off the wall. I kept going down the hall. When I noticed another opening on the same side. I turned and started to go in when Amara suddenly bumped into me. "I guess that was just a distraction," she whispered as she came into the main hall.

As we continued down the passageway, we came across three more tunnels that just led to the main one and two dead ends. We reached the end of the passageway that led to a large door. We pushed the door open just a little to see if there was anyone in the room. As I peered into the room, I didn't see anyone, so we moved in slowly, only opening the door wide enough to slip through.

The room was filled with large pillars placed

evenly throughout the room. We moved to the left of the room and followed the wall while hiding behind the pillars. Suddenly, another large door opened and shut. We stopped immediately, each standing between the wall and a pillar. I peered around and caught a glimpse of two cyclopses. One asked, "How long are we supposed to hold them?"

"Until the human is gone."

"Can we at least eat the troll?"

"No, they must all be left alone. Unless they are here too much longer, we can just say he tried to escape."

I looked over at Amara and motioned for us to keep moving. She nodded and slowly started to move toward the other end of the room. When we reached the other end of the room, I peered out again to see where they were. I spotted them at the corner diagonally from us. While looking, Amara tapped me on the shoulder and pointed to another hallway along the wall opposite the door we entered. We moved slowly to the opening of the hallway and then down the hall. Once we got further down the hall, we began to hear voices screaming to be let out. We moved quickly in the direction of the voices and came to a cell.

Chapter Nineteen

Inside the cell were Valina and the troll who was passed out on the floor. "Where is Reed?" I whispered. Valina jumped up and ran to the bars of the cell.

"He is over there," she said as she pointed to a large glass jar with a few air holes poked into it sitting just outside the cell.

"We have to get you out of here. We saw two cyclopses out in the big room. Have you seen anyone else?" I asked.

"No, they come in every so often to shake Reed's jar in our faces and then leave," replied Valina.

"Did they bring you here through the falls, or is there another way out of here?" asked Amara.

Muffled from the jar Reed replied, "There is another way out. I think I can lead the way if you can get us out of here."

I reached down and opened up the jar Reed was being held in. He flew out and began trying to pick the large iron lock to the cell. Suddenly, the lock fell onto the ground making a loud noise. "Someone may have heard that; we need to move now," whispered Amara. Valina ran out of the door, but the troll was still knocked out on the ground.

"Remind me to ask our friend's name when he wakes up." I said as I picked up the troll and followed the others down a dark passageway. We came to another room similar to the first large room. The only difference was the size. It was about half the length of the first room.

We stayed at the entrance to the room as Reed flew up toward the ceiling and around the room to see if anyone else was in there. He came back and said, "It's all clear. The door is on the right side of the room." We all moved quickly toward the door when suddenly a cyclops started into the room.

"Hey, get back here." He yelled as he started to chase us, followed by the second one as he entered the room. We ran as fast as we could, making it to the door in time to open it and close it before we were caught. Once in the hallway we came upon a staircase that lead-up to the ceiling. We followed it up to a door just when the first cyclops reached the stairs. Reed moved out of the way, as Valina rammed the ceiling with her shoulder. After a few hits, the door opened.

We ran out and shut the door behind us. We looked around for something to place on top of the door. We found a large rock that Valina and Amara rolled on top of the door. "We should keep moving into the woods before they figure a way out," said Reed.

Chapter Twenty

We rushed into the woods just as they managed to open the door. We kept going until we could not hear the falls anymore. Luckily, the trees were dense enough that the cyclops could not follow us. We all stopped and sat down to rest. I opened up the satchel, grabbed a piece of food, and passed the bag so everyone else could eat too. The troll was still passed out leaning up against a tree. Valina noticed me just watching him lay there.

"They enjoyed knocking him around," she said as

she placed her hand on my shoulder. She said, "By the way, his name is Lomgan." I smiled at her as I placed my hand on hers.

"Is he going to be all right?" I asked.

"I don't know. If he is not awake, by the time we get to town, we will take him straight to the doctor," Amara replied.

After we all got a little rest, we were once

again on our way. We moved slowly through the trees with Reed and Amara in the lead. I was following them with Lomgan in my arms, and Valina brought up the rear. It was still light when we reached the lake, so we stopped for a drink and to splash our faces. However, we did not stay long. We moved around the edge of the lake until we reached the other side and ran into the forest just as it was getting dark but not before we saw a mothman in the sky.

"Do you think he saw us?" I asked as we began to move faster.

"Not sure, but I don't really want to find out," replied Amara.

"There has to be a faster way to get through the forest," stated Valina.

Reedstaff

"If we can get to the river we can follow it," replied Reed.

We all agreed and started north toward the river. It did not take too long for us to get to the river. Once we reached the river, we moved faster since we were not weaving in and out of as many trees as before. There was one problem with our being that close to the river; we were not covered as well as we had been in the trees, but all I could see when I looked up every so often were a few dragons.

Suddenly, Reed moved towards the trees again. The rest of us followed with no question. "There are mothmen up ahead," he whispered. We moved further into the woods until we had reached a very dense area of the woods.

"The mothmen cannot get this far into the forest because of their wings; however, some of their friends can," warned Amara.

"How are we to know who is on their side and who is on ours?" I asked.

"There really isn't a way to know; we will just have to be careful. If we are lucky we won't come across anyone," replied Amara.

We moved on through the trees. However, it was taking us a lot longer than we had hoped since we were trying to stay in the thickest part of the forest.

After a few hours of moving through the thick forest, we came across a couple of trolls, a male and female, coming toward us. There was no way we could hide since they had seen us.

"Good evening friends," said the female troll.

"Good evening to you as well," replied Amara.

They did not say anything more as they continued past us and disappeared among the trees. We tried to pick up our pace just in case they were sent to see where we were. As we moved along, we saw lights in the trees up ahead.

"Don't worry they are friendly. My family lives in these trees," whispered Reed.

We all nodded as we moved closer to the lit-up trees.

Chapter Twenty-one

A handful of fairies appeared in front of us.

"Will you help us?" asked Reed.

The other fairies nodded that they could.

Reed and the other fairies worked out a plan that the swarm of fairies would fly out of the woods about a mile away from where we were to distract the mothmen, and we would continue on to the Eastern Gate.

It began to look like daylight within the woods as fairies swarmed all around us. We moved forward with them until we could just see the end of the forest. Then the swarm moved away from us to become our distraction. We moved quickly, knowing that we had little time to get to the gate. Just as we entered the clearing, we noticed the mothmen were flying away. That was until we were about half way to the gate when we were spotted by a mothman. They began flying directly at us, swooping down to try to get us. Any time they got close to getting one of us, the others in our group would throw stones that we found on the ground at the mothman as the one they were going after ran as fast as they could.

We made it to the gate just as four mothmen flew towards us at once. However, when they saw we had reached the gate, they stopped because they knew what creature was guarding the Eastern Gate. When I looked ahead of us, there were two large animals in front of us. Amara informed me that they were chimeras. They had three heads, a goat, a dragon, and a lion. Their bodies looked like a lions with wings of a dragon, feet of a goat, and tails of snakes, with its head at the end. We all moved forward past the Chimeras and into the town. Amara took Lomgan from my arms as she said, "Don't worry; I will get him to the doctor as fast as I can."

I nodded as she turned around with Lomgan and bumped right into Anna. "Is your friend all right, Amara?" asked Anna.

"Anna you can get there faster. Can you please take

Lomgan to the doctor?" asked Amara.

"Yes, right away," replied Anna as she took Lomgan and ran in the direction of the doctor.

Chapter Twenty-Two

As Valina, Reed, Amara and I slowly walked toward the doctor's, knowing we were all safe within the walls, we smiled at each other. Just then something ran up behind me and nudged me in the back. I turned around to see Chip. I wrapped my arms around his neck while the others continued on ahead. Then Chip said, "You're safe. You're safe. I knew you would be. See everyone; see, I told you she would be safe."

I squeezed him tighter knowing what he said was true; I was safe. When I let go of Chip's neck, I noticed Anna standing beside him. "Welcome back my friend. We were worried you had been killed until the wovels at the gate told us they had seen you. Do not worry now that you are here. No one will try to kidnap you again. You see they thought they could keep humans out by killing you and making us believe you attacked them. The only thing they were not aware of is that we had already gotten to know that you could never hurt us. Oh, and do not worry; Lomgan is with the doctor."

"Thank you Anna for not giving up on me and also for getting Lomgan to the doctor as fast as you did." I said, as I hugged her. While looking at Chip and Anna, I asked, "Can one of you take me to the doctor's? I would like to see how Lomgan is doing."

"I can. I can take you there. You look tired; hop on." replied Chip. I hopped onto his back, and we were off to the doctor's to see if Lomgan was all right.

When we reached the doctors, I slipped down off of Chip's back. "I'll wait out here," he said as I opened the door to the building. When I got inside

I saw Valina, Reed and Amara in front of a bed. When I came up between them, I saw Lomgan in the bed smiling up at me.

"Maybe I should have gone with you when you left my place my friend," said Lomgan.

I smiled as I asked, "Are you going to be all right?"

"Yes. I'm just a bit sore. Thank you, by the

way, for saving me and carrying me all the way here." I smiled and hugged him.

"We should get you home Mena," said Amara.

"Will I be able to return and visit all of you?" I asked as we all headed out the door to where Chip was standing.

"Yes, and now that we know there is a chance that humans can accept magic once again, more of us will be able to travel to your world as well." said Amara.

"Trank, the mothman that kidnapped Mena, planned to destroy the stone building that Mena came through," said Valina.

"Yep. Yep. They did. It's just a pile of rubble now," replied Chip.

"That's all right I will take her through the tree that I go through when

I leave the realm" replied Amara.

I hugged each of my new friends and told them I would return as soon as I could.

Chapter Twenty-Three

Amara and I walked to a small collection of trees just inside the city near the eastern gate. "If you go through the tree there in the middle, you will end up back in the forest in Selpan," she said, pointing to the trees.

"Will you come visit me some time?"

"Every chance I am able to. Plus you will be able to visit us," she replied.

"What will happen to everyone who doesn't want our worlds to merge?"

"Don't worry, most of them will change their

minds, knowing that it will happen no matter what they do. I expect that the next time you come, you will be greeted by a warmer welcome from them."

I smiled. "Thank you for everything Amara. If it were not for you, I would still be lost in the woods."

"No, thank you. You have given us all hope that

some day we will no longer need this realm," she said, as she hugged me.

I turned toward the tree and started to walk away and then I quickly turned back around. "Amara, what do I tell my parents? How can I explain why I have been gone so long?"

"Time in our realm does not match up with time in your world. In your world, you have only been gone a few hours, not days," she replied. I smiled and waved good-bye as I walked into the tree.

Chapter Twenty-four

When I came out the other side, I wanted to prove I was not dreaming, so I popped my head back in for a moment to make sure I could return. When I did, I saw Amara walking away. Pulling my head out of the tree, I noticed it was still raining. I started up the hill back toward my house. Once I reached the top of the hill, I began to run to the house. I opened the front door and saw my parents sitting asleep on the couch. I sat in the chair across from them and fell asleep myself.

Suddenly, my mother was shaking me awake. "Mena, where on Earth have you been?"

"I am sorry. I tried to stay out of the rain in an old tree and fell asleep. When I woke up it was still raining so I waited for it to slow a bit. When it did, I came right home." They hugged me and sent me off to bed.

As I walked up the stairs, I heard my mom ask my dad "Where did she get that dress?"

"No clue," he responded.

I looked down and realized I had forgotten to change before I left. I smiled at the little bit of proof I had that I was not dreaming.

About the Author

Krystal A. Erbelding was born in Canandaigua New York, in 1986. She currently lives in Kentucky with her mother and her three pets. When Krystal is not writing she enjoys cooking and knitting.

www.ingramcontent.com/pod-product-compliance
Lightning Source LLC
Chambersburg PA
CBHW022059170626
46808CB00002B/512